Growing Up Daisy

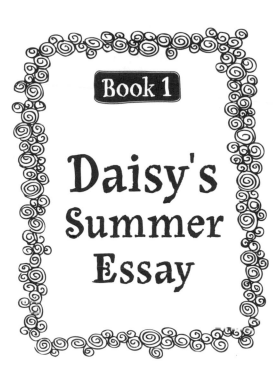

Book 1

Daisy's Summer Essay

By: Marci Peschke

Illustrated by: M.H. Pilz

magic wagon

visit us at www.abdopublishing.com

To Para Mis Amigas: Deborah, Elizabeth & Mary Beth - MP
For Dave - MHP

Printed in the United States of America, Melrose Park, Illinois.
092010
012011
 This book contains at least 10% recycled materials.

Original text by Marci Peschke
Illustrated by M.H. Pilz
Edited by Stephanie Hedlund and Rochelle Baltzer
Cover and interior design by Abbey Fitzgerald

Library of Congress Cataloging-in-Publication Data

Peschke, M. (Marci)
  Daisy's summer essay / by Marci Peschke ; illustrated by
M.H. Pilz.
     p. cm. -- (Growing up Daisy ; bk. 1)
  ISBN 978-1-61641-114-5
  [1. Schools--Fiction. 2. Mexican Americans--Fiction.] 1. Pilz,
MH, ill. 11. Title.
  PZ7.P441245Dd 2011
  [Fic]--dc22
                                    2010028460

Table of Contents

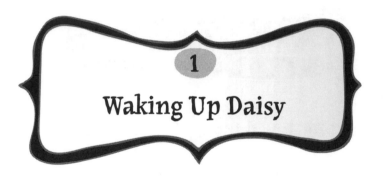

1
Waking Up Daisy

Daisy Martinez lived in a loud house. It was always filled with laughter and noise. There were no quiet places in the white house with trim as blue as the sky.

Daisy was the oldest of the Martinez kids. She shared her room with her *hermana* Paola and her *abuela* Lupe.

The room next to hers was shared by her twin *hermanos* Manuel and Diego. Every night her new baby sister Carmen slept between her parents in their own room. All of the bedrooms were upstairs.

Downstairs, Mami was already busy cooking in the kitchen when Daisy woke up. Today she was making a special breakfast. It was the first day of school after the long summer.

The smell of cinnamon filled the air. Mami would serve banana *empanadas* with milk and juice. Daisy could hear Manuel and Diego fighting over the first plate.

Boys, she thought, *they're always eating too much and not thinking enough.* Daisy knew this because Manuel and Diego never made good grades at school like she and Paola did.

Paola was already getting ready for school. Paola was younger and only in the second grade. With all of her family around her Daisy was never ever alone and she liked it that way.

When it was time to get ready, Daisy let Abuela brush her long, black hair until it was shiny. Then, she felt her grandmother's hands quickly make one long braid down her back.

"Hurry, *mi ja*," Abuela said, "or you will not get any breakfast. You know how your brothers like to eat!"

Daisy knew it was true, so she hurriedly pulled on a tan jumper. Then, she put on hot pink socks and black high-top tennis shoes with the tops rolled down.

She finished by putting a hot pink daisy at the top of her braid and a hot pink band at the bottom of it. Then she looked in the mirror.

Daisy saw a ten-year-old girl who was not short, but not too tall either. Her eyes were light brown, her hair was black, and her skin was the color of warm caramel.

Daisy knew her face was round. In fact she was a little round all over. She knew she was not a skinny stick like some of the girls at school, but that was okay with her. She thought she looked very beautiful and that everyone at school would wish they had hot pink socks, too!

After Daisy was ready, she ran downstairs and quickly ate breakfast. Then, it was time to leave for school.

Daisy stepped outside into a blast of hot air. Even early in the morning it was hot like an oven in Townsend, Arizona.

Her brothers were already walking far ahead of her. Paola lagged behind them all.

Paola followed Daisy a lot and wanted to be just like her big sister. If Daisy said that she loved watermelon bubble gum, which she did, then Paola said she loved it, too. Every time Daisy snuggled up with her little dog Noche, then Paola wanted to hold Noche.

Daisy called, "Hurry, Paola, or you will be late on your first day!" Sometimes it was hard to be the big sister, but Daisy knew it was important for her to look after her siblings.

Daisy began walking as slow as a snail so Paola could catch up with her.

As she walked, Daisy noticed the neat rows of houses where her neighbors lived. Her *tia* Louisa lived two houses down. Her other tia, Maria, lived two streets over. She turned the corner and stood in front of her school.

The new building gleamed in the early morning sun. The sign in front of the school said, "Welcome back, Townsend Elementary Tigers!" Daisy tossed her new black book bag with silver hearts over her shoulder and stepped inside.

The hall was cool. Kids were crammed inside, all pushing to get to class. Some kids were standing in front of their lockers.

Across the hall, a girl was waving at Daisy. Daisy rushed through the kids in the hall until she was in front of her best friend in the whole wide world.

"I have some watermelon bubble gum. Want some?" Daisy asked.

Blanca replied, "I have some *big* news! We have the new teacher."

Blanca had short, curly black hair and nice brown eyes. Today she was wearing a pair of Capri pants and a white blouse.

"Really? I can't believe it!" Daisy said.

Daisy and Blanca were worried they would get Ms. Smith. No one wanted to be in her class because she liked teaching with worksheets and she was a tough teacher.

Daisy followed her best friend to room 210. As they went inside, Daisy smiled—she was 10 in room 210. It was a sign. She liked signs.

Suddenly, a boy stuck his foot out. Daisy tripped a little, but she didn't care because she knew signs were lucky. Her last year in elementary school was going to be a great year!

Inside, Daisy found her seat. She got to sit across from Blanca.

Then, her eyes wandered around the room. On the board were neat, curly letters that said *Welcome to 4th Grade! Ms. Lilly.*

Daisy noticed the brightly colored beanbag chairs and the beaded curtain in the reading corner. She saw the "School is Cool" bulletin board with markers to write your thoughts. She looked at the supply table with glitter, markers, and a huge pile of rainbow paper.

What she didn't see yet was Ms. Lilly. But she already knew that she was going to like her teacher.

2

Meeting Ms. Lilly

The kids in room 210 talked, shouted, and passed notes. No one was paying attention as a tall woman with wild, black, curly hair stepped in the room.

Daisy was the first to notice the woman. She was wearing a long, purple dress and about a hundred beaded necklaces. She had a pair of sparkly red glasses on one of her necklaces.

This must be Ms. Lilly, Daisy thought.

Ms. Lilly stepped quickly inside the classroom and pulled the door shut behind her. Lifting the glasses to her eyes, she looked around the room. It got so quiet you could hear some kids breathing.

Finally Ms. Lilly said, "Hellooo, class. I am so excited. I have great news. You are all super smart superstars!" Then she smiled and crossed the room to her desk.

The new teacher did not sit down like other teachers. Later, they would all learn that Ms. Lilly almost never sat down. Instead, she pulled a marker from her drawer and wrote on the board in lime green ink: *It is our reading time! No talking, just reading. Begin now!*

All of the kids looked around the room. Daisy looked around. Even the mean boy who tripped her looked around with bored eyes.

After all, it was the first day and the students of room 210 did not even have school books yet. They definitely didn't have a reading book!

Ms. Lilly pulled a book from her book bag and began reading as she walked around the room. Daisy wondered if being a super smart superstar would give her superpowers.

Surely I have the power to find a book, Daisy thought.

Beside her in the reading corner were shelves packed with paperback books. Quietly, Daisy stood up and made her way to the bookshelves. She picked a book with a bright pink cover.

Today will be a positively pink day, she decided.

The book was perfect. It was about a girl who was going to a new school and next year Daisy would be going to middle school. The girl in the book was feeling a little anxious just like Daisy.

Ms. Lilly suddenly stopped walking, shocking everyone who thought she was just reading. She pointed straight at Daisy.

Daisy held her breath and hoped her superpowers were fully activated. She did not want to get into trouble on the first day of fourth grade.

Ms. Lilly shouted, "Bravo, dear girl! Well done indeed. You need a book to read a book. What is your name?"

Daisy smiled and said, "I'm Daisy Martinez."

Then Ms. Lilly said, "Everyone, follow Daisy's lead and quietly get a book."

Daisy made her way back to her desk through the kids who were crowding around to get a book. She sat down and opened the book she'd chosen.

Ms. Lilly walked back and forth in the front of the room. She was reading and watching as each student found a book and began to read.

Finally, every student was reading except the boy who had looked bored before. He still had his legs stuck out in the aisle between the desks. His arms were crossed and his eyes were closed. He didn't see Ms. Lilly in front of him, even though she looked right at him.

Then Ms. Lilly laid down the book she had been reading on his desk and whispered in his ear. The boy, whose name was Raymond, sat up. He opened his eyes, but he did not pick up the book on his desk.

Is he loco? *You would have to be little crazy not to want to read the teacher's book,* Daisy thought. *I'd be happy to just read the title of the book. Maybe then I could check it out at the school library.*

Ms. Lilly was looking at Raymond. Her big, green cat eyes stared at him until he picked up the book.

Blanca leaned over and whispered to Daisy, "What do you think she said in his ear?"

Daisy shrugged and said, "Who knows."

She had no idea what Ms. Lilly said. No one knew, but everyone knew Raymond. And they knew he didn't like teachers, school, or reading!

Daisy thought the only thing that could get Raymond to read was Ms. Lilly's superpowers. She made a mental note to find out how to make boys follow directions. This would be a very useful superpower with two younger brothers at home!

Before long, it was time for lunch. The cafeteria sounded noisy like gym class. Everyone was talking about Ms. Lilly. Even the kids who had the other fourth grade teachers were asking, "Is it true that she didn't give out reading books? Is it true that she made *Raymond* read a book?"

Some kids said she must have hypnotized him. Daisy decided that if her teacher really did hypnotize Raymond with her green eyes, she couldn't use that power on her brothers. After all, she didn't have green eyes.

Daisy was sitting with Blanca, Min, and DeShaye. Mami said that Min always talked like a grown-up. DeShaye was a really good tennis player. She even had a coach and went to competitions.

Daisy had a new black lunch bag with bright, rainbow-colored peace signs on it. She pulled her lunch out. Then she announced, "I have spicy rice."

Across the table, Min pulled her lunch out. She said," I have rice, too." They both laughed. Blanca and DeShaye had school lunches. Daisy thought the chocolate chip cookie on Blanca's tray looked yummy!

"Hey, Blanca," Daisy said. "I'm your very best friend, so gimme some of your cookie, pleeease?"

Blanca broke it in half and shared it with Daisy. After Daisy thanked her, she listened as Blanca told Min and DeShaye about Ms. Lilly's reading corner.

When Blanca finished her story, Min told everyone about her morning in Mrs. Smith's room.

"She's pretty nice, but not as cool as Ms. Lilly," Min said.

"You're all sooo lucky!" DeShaye said. "I have Mr. Harrison, who has gray hair. And instead of smiling, his mouth looks like he's been biting a lemon. He gave us homework already and it's not even the end of the first day!"

Daisy said, "My abuela has gray hair, and she's sweet."

They all agreed with Daisy. Then, they decided that none of the other teachers could ever be as awesome as Ms. Lilly.

Soon, the warning bell rang signaling that lunch was over. As the girls cleared their table, Daisy noticed Raymond at the end of their table with two lunch trays. Blanca noticed, too.

Blanca quietly said, "Was he listening to us talk about our teachers?"

DeShaye shook her head and said, "No way, he was too busy eating to listen."

"Oh, who cares if he heard us," Daisy said. "No one said anything terrible, so we can't get in trouble for it."

On the way back to class, Daisy waved to her mami. Mami worked half days as a clerk in the school office. Mami smiled and waved back.

3

Daisy's Surprises

Tap . . . tap . . . tap . . . Ms. Lilly's foot tapped while she waited impatiently for her students to put their things in their lockers. Soon, they were all waiting in a long line that snaked down the hall.

"Are you ready, students?" Ms. Lilly asked.

Daisy thought it was a mysterious question. They had only been gone for lunch after all. What did they need to be ready for? Everyone was quiet.

Suddenly, Raymond shocked them all. From his place at the very end of the line he said, "Yes!"

Ms. Lilly laughed. Then she said, "Marvelous, just marvelous. Please do come right in."

She held the door open. Daisy blinked. Room 210 had been transformed.

While they were at lunch, Ms. Lilly had been busy! In one corner was a huge, fake palm tree.

Blanca pointed and said, "Look over there."

Daisy saw a large, colorful beach umbrella with beach towels and a picnic basket. Bright posters with pictures from other countries covered the walls.

Daisy giggled and pointed at the poster with the Eiffel Tower on it. Across the front it said, "Bonjour!"

Daisy said, "Oooh, I just love the Eiffel Tower." Blanca nodded to say she did, too.

Raymond was standing in front of a poster from Spain with a bullfighter on it. Blanca raced across the room to check out the "Disney is Magic" poster. It had a huge castle on it and a princess.

Suddenly, Daisy realized that music was playing. At first it sounded strange. She listened to the music and it got a little better.

Ms. Lilly leaned over and said, "It's the bagpipes. They play them in Scotland. Everywhere in the room are souvenirs from faraway places."

Then, Daisy noticed that every desk had something on it. She ran to her desk and found a large box. She carefully opened the box to discover a white teapot with pink roses was inside.

Ms. Lilly came by Daisy's desk. Her *maestra* picked up the teapot and said, "The English people are so smart. I do love afternoon tea."

Daisy was trying to think of something clever to say. Before she could, Ms. Lilly moved to the front of the room and clapped three times. The class was learning that this meant they should be quiet and pay attention.

Madison was hissing like a snake. *"Sssh! Sshh!"* she said. Madison was one of the popular girls in fourth grade.

Blanca leaned over to Daisy and said, "She thinks she's the boss, but she's not!"

Ms. Lilly said, "Now that I have your attention, we are about to begin a journey."

Madison's friend Lizzie passed out little blue folders with golden eagle stickers on the front. They were passports. Inside them there were places to put travel stuff.

Daisy was so excited she couldn't wait any longer. She raised her hand and even waved it a little.

Ms. Lilly said, "Daisy, do you have a question?"

Daisy asked, "What are we going to do with these passports?"

Ms. Lilly explained their writing assignment. The students would write an essay about their summer vacation and then fill the little passport with information and pictures that went with the essay.

Blanca sent Daisy a note that said, "This is kind of like a project."

Daisy wrote under Blanca's note, "*Sí!* I love projects!" Then she passed it back to Blanca.

Madison, Lizzie, and some of the other kids were talking about their vacations. Madison had gone to England with her dad, who had work to do in London. Madison's vacation made Daisy think about Ms. Lilly's teapot.

Lizzie had gone to Disney World. Another classmate had gone on a cruise. Someone else went to Alaska. It seemed like almost everyone had gone someplace really special. A few kids just went to visit their grandparents or stayed in the city.

Blanca said, "I call Mexico!"

"Okay," Daisy said. She had gone to Mexico too, but she didn't want to write about the same place as Blanca.

The bell rang while Daisy was trying to think of the best place she had been over the summer. Kids were loading up their backpacks and heading for the door. Daisy piled her books into her black *mochila* with silver hearts.

Blanca waved at Daisy and said, "Call me tonight and we can talk about our essays."

Daisy called back, "TTYL."

It would be much later before Daisy could call Blanca. She would have to wait until after dinner. Mami insisted that she and her brothers all help with the evening meal.

Daisy's job that night was to cut melon into nice little squares. Then, she put the melon in a big blue bowl and sprinkled chili spice on it. The melon would taste cool against the heat of the chili. Everyone at the table would want to eat more!

Abuela helped Mami make fresh, hot tortillas. Mami's food smelled spicy. Yum!

Manuel and Diego put the silverware and dishes on the table. The plates were bright and colorful.

Paola went to the backyard to cut flowers to put in a vase in the middle of the table. Carmen sat in her baby seat making noises that sounded like singing. Everyone was doing their part.

Soon they all heard the truck in the driveway. Papi was home! He came to the kitchen smiling at Mami. He kissed her cheek. Then he sang a little song for Carmen about a tiny chicken. Carmen laughed.

After that he said, "How are my other girls tonight?" Daisy and Paola both said, "*Muy bueno.*"

Abuela looked up from rolling tortillas. She said, "Jorge, I am no girl."

"No," Papi said. "But you cook like an angel, and I am really hungry!"

The whole Martinez family sat at the big kitchen table together. Papi said a little prayer and everyone began to talk at once about their day. The food was passed around the table so they could all fill their plates.

Mami announced, "I have a new *patrón!* Townsend Elementary has a new principal named Mr. Donaldson."

Daisy said, "He was in the cafeteria today and he didn't yell or anything. So, he must like kids."

Manuel whined, "I have two pages of homework already."

Diego complained, "Me too! And it's the first day of school!"

Paola said, "I wish I had papers to do, too."

The brothers filled their plates with second helpings. Paola pulled on Mami's sleeve, pointing at the boys' plates.

Mami said, "We have plenty to eat and your brothers seem to be really hungry!" She told Papi that Manuel's school pants would be too short soon.

Abuela said, "Don't worry. I will make them into shorts." Abuela was always sewing something. Her hands were steady and her stitches were tiny and neat. Some people paid her to hem their pants.

At Daisy's house everything was used and used again. Old clothes were passed around or Abuela would make something new out of them. Mami said every time they used something twice it was better for the family and better for the planet.

At the end of the meal Papi asked, "Who does the dishes tonight? Boys or girls?"

Daisy shouted, "Boys!" She was glad it was the boys' turn. She wanted to call Blanca. She dialed the number and waited as it rang.

"*Bueno*," said Blanca's mami.

Daisy said, "*Hola*, Senora Vasquez. May I please talk to Blanca?" Then she heard Blanca's mami calling her to come to the phone.

Blanca was excited! She did not even say hello. She said, "I've already started to write my essay."

Daisy was a little jealous, because she didn't even have a single word for her paper yet.

Blanca asked her, "How many paragraphs do you have?"

"Help me, Blanca!" Daisy begged. "I can't decide what to write about. You're writing about Mexico and we can't write about the same place!"

Blanca told Daisy to make a list of all of the places she went over the summer.

"That is a great idea!" Daisy agreed. They talked all about their first day, Ms. Lilly, and seeing DeShaye and Min.

Finally Daisy said, "Blanca, I gotta go. I have to do my other homework."

As she walked down the hall, she heard her mother's soft, clear voice singing:

El sol es de oro
la luna es de plata
y las estrellitas
son de hoja de lata.

In English the words said,

"The sun's a gold medallion,
the moon's a silver ball,
the little stars are only tin,
I love them best of all."

The lullaby meant that Carmen was going to sleep. Her parents made sure all of the kids were getting ready for bed.

While the boys brushed their teeth Papi came to her door and said, "Daisy, your bedtime is nine o'clock now. You're in fourth grade, so you'll need the time since you'll have *mucho* homework."

Then Papi winked at her. He kissed her on the top of her head and went to see why Manuel and Diego weren't done brushing yet.

4

"Daisy" Socks

The next day at school, Ms. Lilly said, "Students, to get you started on your essays, tomorrow I want each of you to bring a summer souvenir. We will have some show-and-tell time. You can bring a picture, a shell, or something you bought—anything from your summer adventure!"

Then she wrote on the board in orange marker under assignments: *Bring something to share from your summer!*

Daisy heard Madison brag to Lizzie, "I bet most of the kids in our class bring something cheap or stupid. My souvenir will be the best. I just know it!"

Daisy shook her head. She whispered to Blanca, "Madison always has to be better than everyone else. Sometimes I just can't stand it!"

Daisy looked at Madison. She had light brown hair in a ponytail and was wearing tan shorts, a white shirt, and white tennis shoes. Her face was pretty, but she was sour on the inside.

Abuela always said, "It is important to be sweet inside like sugar. If you are sour like a pickle no one will like you." Daisy thought that her abuela was right. Madison was not a very nice girl. Sometimes, she was really mean.

Daisy looked at Blanca, who was listening to Madison and Lizzie, too. Blanca rolled her eyes. Then they both laughed.

Lizzie asked, "What's so funny, Daisy?"

Daisy answered, "Oh nothing, nothing at all." Then she looked at Blanca and they both giggled again.

Just then Ms. Lilly saved the day by telling the class to get ready for lunch. Daisy was pretty sure Ms. Lilly had used her superpowers to listen to those other girls brag on and on. She decided Ms. Lilly wanted those girls to stop bragging just as much as she and Blanca did.

At the lunch table, Daisy and Blanca met Min and DeShaye. Daisy opened her lunch bag and said, "Mmmm! I have tamales made with veggies."

Min laid down her chopsticks and said, "I have stir fry made with veggies." They both laughed.

Min said, "I don't think we'll bring the same food every day all year. That would be really odd, but so far it has been really fun!"

Daisy nodded to agree with Min. Then she noticed that Raymond was sitting at the end of their table again.

DeShaye asked, "Doesn't that boy have any friends of his own?" All of the girls looked down at Raymond, who had four chocolate milks on his tray.

"No, he's kinda weird," Blanca answered.

Then Min said, "Daisy, I just love your colored socks. I'd like to have some."

Daisy was wearing her black shoes with lime green socks today. She had a cheerful green daisy tucked into her long black braid.

"I want some, too!" Blanca said. "We should all get some colorful socks and black shoes." DeShaye agreed excitedly. She told them that she already had a bright yellow pair.

Min said, "From now on, we'll call our colored socks 'Daisy socks'." DeShaye, Min, and Blanca all decided they would wear "Daisy socks" and black shoes on Friday.

Because Ms. Lilly was such a fun teacher, the rest of the day passed super fast. Soon, all of the Martinez kids were walking home. It was so hot outside you could cook an egg on the sidewalk.

When they got home, the Martinezes all rushed inside to get a cool drink of water. Daisy sat down beside her baby sister.

Noche jumped up barking and licked her face. Daisy said, "Hola, Noche!"

Diego started running around the room chanting, "Daisy has dog breath. Daisy has dog breath." Daisy didn't care because she loved her little black dog.

She said, "Noche has better breath than you, Diego!"

Manuel had gone to see what after-school snack their abuela had for them. Abuela brought a plate full of dried fruit and white cheese. Daisy loved the soft, sweet papaya.

"Everyone give me your crunchy banana chips," Diego said. "They're the best."

Daisy gave Diego hers, but Paola wouldn't give him any, because she liked them, too. The boys took the rest of their snack outside.

Daisy and Paola stayed inside, where it was much cooler. They talked to Carmen until Abuela put her in bed for a nap. Then she told Daisy and Paola to go do their homework.

Daisy knew this was the time of day her abuela watched her show on television.

Daisy called, "Noche, come!" She wanted her dog to keep her company while she worked. Noche barked and ran after the girls.

In her room, Daisy took out several pieces of clean, smooth, white paper and a box of colored pens. She sat at the desk she and Paola shared.

Today it was Paola's turn to sit on the floor and do her work on a little board Papi made for them. It was like a little desk you could put on your lap.

Paola went on and on about her teacher. Daisy didn't mean to be unkind, but she ignored Paola. She already knew all about Paola's teacher, Ms. Wall, because she had her for second grade, too. Daisy had work to do.

Instead of listening to her sister, she had been writing. Across the top of her paper she wrote in green ink: *Summer Vacation List*. Then she stopped.

What could she write on her list? She thought for a moment and then began:

Seeing cousins in Mexico
The IMAX Theater
The King Tut exhibit at the art museum
Riding the Ferris wheel at Navy Pier in
    Chicago
Visiting Papi's family in Michigan
Going to the beach on Lake Michigan
Exploring the Beaver Island Lighthouse
Picking blueberries

Daisy looked at her list and made a dark black line through seeing cousins in Mexico. Daisy already knew that Blanca was writing about Mexico.

Tomorrow she would have to bring something from her summer travels for Ms. Lilly's class. She leaned back on the small desk chair, trying to decide what to bring. It needed to be unique.

"Daisy, can you help me with my math?" Paola asked.

Daisy decided that maybe she was thinking about her homework too much. So she sat down on the floor beside Paola. Daisy helped her sister with multiplication tables until their mami called them to get ready for dinner.

The Search Is On

After dinner and dishes, Daisy went back to her room. She had been thinking all through the noisy meal about what souvenir to bring to school.

Mami suggested that Daisy bring the postcard from the Ferris wheel at Navy Pier. Daisy took it off of the little bulletin board over her desk and put it on her bed. Then, she dug through her desk drawer to find the ticket stubs from the IMAX Theater.

Just then, Paola came in. She asked, "Whatcha doing, Daisy?"

Daisy answered, "This is part of my homework. I need something exciting from our summer."

Paola said, "I can sneak in the boys' room and find the picture Papi took of the lighthouse. Want me to do it?"

Daisy thought for a second. It seemed like more choices would definitely be better, so she agreed. But, she told Paola to be careful—the boys' room was always a disgusting mess.

While Paola was on her mission to get the photo, Mami called, "Daisy, the phone is for you!"

"Who is it?" Daisy asked.

Mami said, "Come and ask them!"

Daisy took the phone from Mami's hand. She said, "Hello?" On the other end of the line she could hear laughing. It was DeShaye talking to her sister. They were always laughing about something.

"DeShaye, is that you?" Daisy asked.

DeShaye said, "Hey girl, what's up?"

Daisy told DeShaye all about trying to find the perfect thing to bring for her homework assignment.

"Well," DeShaye said, "it better be good or Madison and Lizzie will make a big deal over it. You know how they like to talk bad about anyone who isn't in their little group."

Daisy said, "Oh, I know! Madison has already been talking about how her souvenir will be the best."

They talked for a while about the way Madison, Lizzie, and their friends always had to be the best at everything.

DeShaye said, "It's cool to be the best sometimes. That's how I won all my tennis trophies and medals. But nobody is perfect all the time. Right, Daisy?"

Daisy agreed.

DeShaye asked, "Whatcha got that you could bring?"

Daisy listed the few items on her bed. Paola successfully found the lighthouse picture in record time and was sitting on the bed swinging her legs.

"Not the ticket stubs!" DeShaye said. "That would be sort of lame. Go for the postcard or the picture, I guess."

"Okay, the stubs are out!" Daisy said.

DeShaye said, "Hate to leave you, but Daddy just brought home ice cream. And I love ya, girl, but . . ."

Daisy laughed, "I know, you love ice cream more, right?"

DeShaye was already hanging up, but first she told Daisy, "Rocky Road, gotta go!"

Daisy went to the closet and opened the door. She stood there for a few minutes, expecting something to jump out at her. Suddenly, it did!

On the floor was something shiny and golden with a snake's head on the top. It was the pharaoh's hat she got at the King Tut exhibit. She picked it up and was thinking, *Just maybe . . .*

Then she noticed it was torn in two places! Her brothers probably did it.

"Mami," Daisy yelled, "Manuel and Diego are tearing up my stuff again! I can't have anything with those loco brothers around."

Daisy was holding the ripped hat so Mami could see it. Mami looked really tired. It had been a long day. Since it was the first week of school Mr. Donaldson had a lot of papers for her to sort and file.

Papi got up from his chair. He said, "I'll take care of it, Claudia." He asked Daisy if Abuela could fix it.

She said, "Papi, it's dirty too, and we can't wash it." Papi went to the boys' room and when he came back he had the handheld video game her brothers shared. He put it on top of the refrigerator.

He looked at Daisy and said, "I told them they can't play with it for a week. And, they will apologize."

The two boys came running into the kitchen, nearly knocking each other over. "Sorry!" they yelled.

"Okay," Daisy said, "but stay *out* of my room from now on. Get it? Keep out! No more boys!"

The sad part was that Daisy still only had the postcard and the picture to choose from. She went to her room and sat on her bed looking at both. They just didn't seem exciting enough.

Soon, Abuela came in and sat on Daisy's bed. She pulled the pins out of the braids that wound around her little head. Papi said that Abuela was shrinking and that all old people shrink.

Abuela shook out her long, grey hair. Looking up she asked, "What's the trouble, mi ja?" She patted a spot on the bed beside her. "Sit here," she said.

Daisy told abuela about her pharaoh's hat and her disappointment. Abuela brushed her hair, and then she took out Daisy's braid and brushed Daisy's hair. Daisy talked for a long time and Abuela listened. Abuela was a good listener.

Finally, Abuela stood and went to her dresser. She pulled out a small, pretty cloth

bag. Daisy wondered what could be inside. She was full of curiosity.

"Abuela, what is it?" Daisy asked.

"Just wait and I will show you," Abuela said. They sat side by side as Abuela pulled open the strings. Out tumbled something sparkly onto her grandmother's lap.

"Ooooh! For me?" Daisy gasped. It was a special bracelet that Daisy recognized at once. It was made from treasures she found on the beach at Lake Michigan.

"Abuela, did you make it?" Daisy asked.

"Yes, I made it just for you," Abuela said. "Now you have something no one else will have at your school. I was going to give it to you for your birthday, but now is a good time. Sí?"

Daisy hugged her Abuela and said, "Sí." Now she was really ready for show-and-tell!

6

Show-and-Tell

It was hard to believe it was Wednesday already. The week was flying by!

For show-and-tell, Blanca brought a *molinillo* from Mexico to show the class. It was a wooden tool used to mix hot chocolate.

"What did you decide to bring?" Blanca asked Daisy.

"I want it to be a surprise," Daisy replied just as Ms. Lilly clapped her hands.

The class quickly quieted. Ms. Lilly was wearing a lot of rings, a red dress, and a scarf with a painting on it. It sort of looked like a kaleidoscope.

"Okay, super smart students," Ms. Lilly said, "I know you have marvelous things to show us and interesting tales to tell. So, let's begin!"

Right away Madison raised her hand, waving it wildly. She shouted, "Ms. Lilly, call on me first!"

Blanca whispered, "Does she always have to be first?"

Daisy leaned across the aisle to her best friend. She said, "Let her go first. We'll all get a turn." Then she said, "I hope I get called on last."

Blanca thought Daisy was being mysterious, just like their teacher was sometimes. Ms. Lilly called on Madison to go first.

Madison moved to the front of the room, proudly carrying a large box. She waited until the room was silent except for the *tick, tick* of the classroom clock.

Finally, Madison looked up with a huge smile. She said, "I'm going to start with my feet. I'm wearing special rain boots from England called Wellies." She pointed at her feet. On them were hot pink rubber boots.

Blanca passed Daisy a note asking if Madison's boots were like the ones at the mall. Daisy wrote, "Hers are from London so I guess they're better than the boots at the mall."

Madison said, "I have a pink umbrella to match them, too!" Some of the boys groaned. Madison continued, "Now I will share my own tiny, English treasure."

Ms. Lilly smiled and said, "I just can't wait to see it, Madison."

Madison opened the flaps of the white box and began to pull out wads of paper one at a time. She commented, "My item is extremely fragile." She pulled paper out of the box for several minutes.

Finally, Jason called out, "Hey, Madison, hurry up!" She pulled something from the box that was wrapped in brown paper. She laid it on the table. Gently she took off the paper revealing a replica of a tall building with a clock on the front. She announced, "This is the world-famous Big Ben!"

From the back of the room Raymond said, "You have got to be joking. We have been waiting forever to see your clock?"

Ms. Lilly said, "Personally, I think Big Ben is a wonderful English treasure. Well done, Madison. Your presentation was charming."

Some other kids gave Madison mean looks. Lizzie started to clap super loud and few other kids clapped, too. Before she could stop herself, Daisy began to clap. She did it because she felt a little sorry for Madison.

Blanca gave her a look like she was a traitor. It was like she was clapping for the enemy. Daisy stopped clapping.

Next, Jason showed a small space shuttle. He went to Junior Space Camp. Several boys shouted, "Cool!" Daisy did not want to take her turn after Jason.

All morning and afternoon kids shared things from their summer travels. Some went to Six Flags, one brought a ticket stub from the IMAX Theater, and another had a golden King Tut face mask.

Daisy was glad she hadn't chosen the IMAX or the art museum ticket stubs. Then, Ms. Lilly called on Blanca.

Blanca went to the front of the room. She told the class that her cousins lived in a beautiful town called San Miguel de Allende, Mexico.

She explained that every morning her tia would make thick chocolate for them to drink. She would use a molinillo to make the dark milk light and foamy on the top.

From the back of the room Raymond said, "Mmmm." Daisy guessed he could not help himself. She remembered the four chocolate milk cartons on his tray.

Blanca held up the molinillo and said, "I'm passing it around so you can all look at it." Daisy clapped extra hard for Blanca and from the back of the room Raymond whistled.

Ms. Lilly smiled at Blanca. Then she clapped.

Once Ms. Lilly had the whole class's attention she said, "Sadly we are out of time. Don't worry, students. The rest of you will get your turn tomorrow. Please gather your things together. The bell is about to ring."

Daisy was not worried. She was actually happy that her turn would have to wait for another day.

"Well, you might get your wish after all," Blanca said. "Since you have to wait, you could be last."

7

The Best for Last

On Thursday, Daisy wore her blue socks and a blue flower in her hair. She wanted to match her souvenir. She pushed some of her books into the locker in front of her.

Min crossed the hall, looking curious. She said, "Hi, Daisy. Blanca told me today you'll share your special summer souvenir. What did you bring?"

Daisy replied, "I have something that was thrown away, but can be used, and it is both old and new at the same time."

Min chewed the end of her pencil. She said, "Oh, I just love a good riddle!" Then she tapped her pencil on her notebook. She said, "I hope to have it figured out by lunch."

DeShaye joined them. She said, "Hey girl, please tell me you did not bring that IMAX ticket for your presentation today, because it is L-A-M-E!"

Then she smiled and told them that she was getting new Daisy socks and a pair of black high-top shoes after school. "I just have to be ready for tomorrow," she said.

"I'll be ready, too," Min said. "I have hot pink socks, but my mom says I can wear my old black shoes."

The bell rang, so the girls went quickly to class. Blanca was already in Ms. Lilly's room waiting for Daisy.

"Hola, *amiga*," Daisy said. "Where were you? Min, DeShaye, and I were talking at the lockers."

Blanca explained that she thought she was going to be late, so she just came straight to class. Blanca's brother was in trouble all last year for being tardy. Blanca didn't want to get into trouble for being late!

Ms. Lilly clapped her hands. The class quietly looked up for directions. Their teacher said, "You have all impressed me with your fantastic treasures. We only have three more students." She looked to the back of the room and called, "Raymond."

Raymond shook his head no. Ms. Lilly said, "Please, Raymond. I just know you have something in your backpack to show us."

Raymond muttered and pulled something out of his bag. It was a giant chocolate bar wrapper. It looked kind of torn up. Raymond walked to the front of the room, held up the brown paper with silvery letters, and walked back to his seat and sat down.

Ms. Lilly said, "Kudos to Raymond for coming to school prepared!"

Daisy took a deep breath. Would she be next?

No! Ms. Lilly called on Lizzie. Before going to the front of the room, Lizzie pushed her princess tiara firmly down on her head.

Soon, Lizzie was telling the class about her trip to Florida. She talked for what seemed like an hour about how hot it is there in the summer. Then she went on and on about the long lines at Disney World. She told the class she hated waiting.

In a loud voice Raymond said, "Me too! I've been waiting to see what Daisy brought."

Daisy's wish finally came true when Ms. Lilly called her last. She was so excited that she felt like a movie star. Everyone was looking at her. The front of the classroom was like a stage.

In her hand, Daisy had a bright cloth bag with a beautiful design sewn on it. It had two strings at the top with beads on the ends that you pulled to open and close the bag.

Daisy waited for a few moments, and then she repeated the riddle she told Min earlier.

"I have something that was thrown away, but can be used, and it is both old and new at the same time," she announced.

Madison complained, "Daisy, just show us what's in the bag. Your riddle is too hard to figure out."

"I like to think," Amber said. "This is fun. It must be from a long time ago if it is old."

Jason raised his hand. When Ms. Lilly called on him, he said, "A lot of people make stuff out of trash or things that get thrown away. They even make houses out of trash. I read about it in my science magazine."

While the entire class watched, Daisy pulled a gleaming silver bracelet out of the bag. It shimmered as she held it up. Then the class saw pieces of frosty blue and green glass that were connected by small, perfectly round stones.

"Wow!" Lizzie said. Madison told her to be quiet.

Daisy explained, "When I visited my family in Michigan, we went to the lake. As we walked along the sand, I picked up the frosty bits of sky blue and jade green glass. It was really fun, like being on a treasure hunt."

Blanca raised her hand. When Ms. Lilly called on her, she said, "I can't believe they would throw away something so beautiful." The girls all agreed the bracelet was really special.

Raymond asked, "Okay, I don't get it. What's so old about it?"

Daisy began to walk around the room so each kid could get a closer look at the bracelet on her wrist.

"The round stones I found on the beach are fossils from the time of the dinosaurs," Daisy explained. "I didn't find them until the second week of my vacation. There was a man on the beach hunting for them, so he told me all about the dino fossils."

Jason raised his hand and said, "May I have permission to get up, Ms. Lilly? I gotta see those fossils up close and I can't wait." Ms. Lilly nodded.

Right when Daisy passed the last desk, the bell rang. Ms. Lilly said, "Daisy, I was mesmerized by your riddle and your unique treasure. I loved everyone's things, but what a fabulous way to end our summer show-and-tell!

"After lunch we will mark our passports and pass them around." Ms. Lilly laughed. She said, "It's like a joke . . . Get it? *Pass* the passports."

At lunch, all anyone could talk about was Daisy's bracelet. The girls' usual table was packed with kids who wanted to look at it. Jason sat by Raymond and Amber sat with them, too.

Blanca told Min and DeShaye, "Raymond brought a giant candy bar wrapper."

DeShaye said, "No way."

Min still couldn't believe that she never got to solve the riddle. Across the cafeteria, Lizzie was still wearing her princess tiara, but everyone had seen them at the party store, so nobody paid any attention to her.

Daisy felt sorry for Lizzie. When she got up to throw away her trash, she stopped to tell Lizzie something.

Daisy said, "Lizzie, I think you are really lucky. Disney World is every kid's dream vacation."

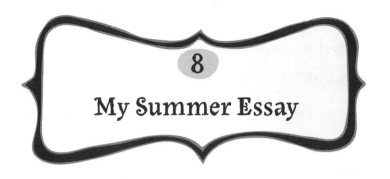

8

My Summer Essay

On Friday morning, the girls all met in front of Daisy's locker. They all smiled and each stuck a foot out for the others to see.

Min had on her hot pink socks. DeShaye was wearing a pair of purple socks. Blanca had on royal blue socks. And, Daisy had red socks to match the flower in her hair.

Min said, "Our feet look like a prism." Min loved science class.

DeShaye disagreed, "No, our feet look amazing. Daisy socks are going to be the coolest thing at school. By next week, everyone will be wearing Daisy socks instead of plain old white ones."

It was almost time for the bell and Daisy still had to get her books out of her locker. She smiled and said, "See you later!"

Daisy spent the morning in Ms. Lilly's class working on an outline for her essay. She barely had any ideas, so it was a bad beginning. Blanca had already sharpened her pencil three times!

Daisy was the peer spelling editor. She got to put her name on the board and the kids who needed to could sign up for her help.

Raymond put his name under hers right away. He came over and handed Daisy his paper. The top of the paper had his name, the date, and *Ms. Lilly* scribbled in messy writing.

"Raymond," Daisy said, "you do know

you have to be writing something to get your spelling checked. Right?" Raymond looked confused for a moment and then wandered back to his seat.

Daisy liked helping the kids in room 210. It made her feel like a teacher, like Ms. Lilly.

That afternoon, Blanca passed Daisy a note. In the note Blanca asked, "Did you notice the look on Madison's face during lunch when Amber said that she was going to wear colored socks and black shoes on Monday?"

Daisy wrote, "No, but I just knew everyone was going to love my socks."

It seemed to Daisy that if a lot of girls started to wear colored socks then Madison would, too.

The afternoon passed and the hands on the clock ticked closer to three. Ms. Lilly said, "Okay, superstar students, you have all weekend to work on your essays. Make them marvelous! They are due Monday."

That night at dinner, Daisy asked everyone about her essay. She said, "I'm writing about our summer vacation, but I'm having a lot of trouble getting started. Can anyone help me?"

Mami said after dinner they could all give her ideas and she could write them down. It was the girls' turn to do dishes. Daisy thought they would never get done.

Finally, Paola dried the last dish and they went to the den. Papi was holding Carmen. When he looked up, he asked, "Where's your paper and pencil, Daisy?"

Daisy dashed off to get them. When she got back, she sat down beside Abuela, who hugged her close. Mami asked everyone to tell Daisy their favorite thing about their vacation.

Abuela said, "I will start. I liked the Farmer's Market. The flowers were *muy bonita* and the vegetables and fruits so fresh!"

Her brothers were fighting over who would go next. Finally, Manuel said, "The Ferris wheel in Chicago was awesome. It was so high you could see across Lake Michigan and the wind was rocking our seat so much I pretended I was going to fall out."

Diego said, "Hey, no fair! That was my favorite, too!" Mami told them they could both choose the ride.

Papi said, "It was good to see my parents, my brother, and his family."

Paola told the family that she loved the white swans they saw when they went to visit the lighthouse.

Then Manuel changed from the Ferris wheel to the haunted lighthouse. He said, "I remember the lady told us that the ghost helped the boats get to land during storms. Anyway, a ghost is better than a ride."

Diego did not agree. He complained that Manuel never even saw the ghost.

Mami finally said, "I will tell you my favorite part now. Riding the train to Chicago was really nice. You could look out the windows and see so many things."

When everyone looked at Carmen, she was already sleeping. So Papi announced it was time for bed and everyone went to their rooms.

The next day, Daisy started writing her essay. She wrote all day on Saturday. Then she had Mami read it to check for mistakes. Sunday she went to church, helped Abuela make a big lunch, and watched a movie.

On Monday when Daisy got to school, Blanca was waiting at the door. She said, "Daisy, I just saw a bunch of girls wearing Daisy socks and black shoes! Min and DeShaye must have told the girls in the other classes about it, too!"

Daisy was super excited. *"Fantástico!"* she exclaimed.

In room 210, a lot of the students were nervous as they turned in their papers. Some kids even forgot theirs.

Daisy noticed that Raymond put a paper in Ms. Lilly's special homework box that said, "You Made Them, I Grade Them!"

Daisy was a little surprised. In the past, Raymond didn't do homework. Daisy decided it must be her teacher's superpower over him.

The day passed quickly. Madison and Lizzie seemed like the only fourth grade girls that were not wearing Daisy socks.

At lunch, all the girls were talking about Daisy socks. They were telling each other where to get the best colors and who had black high-tops on sale. Amber sat at their table again and so did Jason.

Daisy thought that maybe Raymond finally had a friend. Raymond seemed glad to have Jason around. He even offered him one of his chocolate milks.

"Are you sure?" Jason asked.

Raymond nodded and said, "It's cool."

Daisy couldn't wait to tell her family about Daisy socks and her friends that evening.

The next day at school, Daisy noticed that even Madison and Lizzie were wearing Daisy socks and black shoes. She thought it was really awesome.

Daisy walked up to Madison and said, "I really like your socks. Where did you get them?"

Madison said, "At the mall. Have you been to class yet? You need to go look at Ms. Lilly's superstar board."

Daisy ran to room 210. On the board, next to Madison's and Blanca's essays, was Daisy's paper.

Seeing her paper on the board with a big *A+* on the front made Daisy proud. She couldn't wait to tell Mami about her good grade.

My Super Summer Vacation

By Daisy Martinez

Two days riding in a car is a long time, but that is how long it takes to get to Michigan from Arizona. Every summer we visit my papi's family there. We spend long days swimming and collecting special rocks, beach glass, and even fossils at the beach of Lake Michigan.

On Saturday, we went to the Farmer's Market to buy fresh fruit and veggies to make a huge meal. Of course, we bought flowers for the tables, too. There are so many beautiful ones to choose from. They look like a colorful quilt.

One Monday, we rode the train around the lake to Chicago and all along the way we saw interesting things. When we got close to the city, we could see buildings so tall they almost touched the sky.

My brother Diego loved the giant Ferris wheel at Navy Pier. It was too scary for my little sister Paola.

Our next adventure was visiting a haunted lighthouse at Beaver Cove. My brother Manuel loved listening to the tour guide tell spooky stories about the ghost that helped boats get to shore in stormy weather. On the way back, we saw a lake covered with so many white swans it looked like my sister's blue dress with the tiny white dots all over it.

Finally, our trip was over, so we had to say good-bye. We kissed and hugged and kissed and hugged some more, but we were not sad. We knew there would another summer for visiting and for new adventures!

Spanish Glossary

abuela – grandmother

amiga – a female friend

empanada – pie

fantástico – fantastic

hermana – sister

hermano – brother

hola – hello

loco – crazy

maestra – teacher

mi ja – my dear

mochila – backpack

mucho – much or a lot

muy bonita – very pretty

muy bueno – very good

patrón – boss

sí – yes

tia – aunt